Published by Oni-Lion Forge Publishing Group, LLC.

Written by Andrew Cangelose

Illustrated and lettered by Josh Shipley

Edited by Shawna Gore and Grace Scheipeter

❍ ◯ ◉ onipress.com

First Edition: July 2022

ISBN 978-1-63715-045-0

eISBN 978-1-63715-062-7

Library of Congress Control Number: 2021949914

Printed in China.

10 9 8 7 6 5 4 3 2 1

Birthday Cake!

This Is a Disaster!

Words by Andrew Cangelose
Pictures by Josh Shipley

This is a birthday cake.

Cake was first used to celebrate birthdays in the Roman Empire two thousand years ago.

However, they only became widely popular about two hundred years ago during the Industrial Revolution.

Birthday candles became a popular tradition long ago in Germany. The candles were meant to represent the light of life.

Other cultures believed the smoke from the candles carried their prayers and wishes. Many people today make a silent wish as they blow them out.

I WISH we were already partying. Ms. Shelly, this is taking forever. Can I please just start making the cake?

I'm going to make the best cake ever!

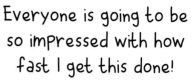

Everyone is going to be so impressed with how fast I get this done!

They'll probably want to throw another party just to celebrate my accomplishment!

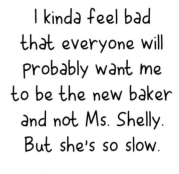

I kinda feel bad that everyone will probably want me to be the new baker and not Ms. Shelly. But she's so slow.

Step 1:

The main ingredient in most cakes is flour. Flour is made by grinding grains into a fine powder.

2 cups of flour

Hmm, rookie mistake ... I forgot to grab the ingredients. But I won't let that slow me down!

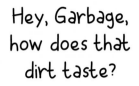
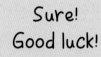

Step 2:

Birthday cakes are traditionally sweetened with sugar. Sugar is harvested from sugar beets and sugarcane. Honey can also be used as a substitute.

1 cup of sugar

Step 3:

The last ingredient in a simple cake needs to be a liquid. This helps the ingredients mix and bind together. Eggs and milk are common options.

1/2 cup of liquid

Step 4:

Mixing cake batter distributes the ingredients so the cake bakes evenly. Overmixing can make the cake too tough and chewy.

Stir slowly for 3 minutes

Step 5:

During the baking process, the cake batter is transformed chemically and physically from goo to fluffy deliciousness.

**Bake at 350 degrees
for 40 minutes**

Steps 6, 7, and 8:

Decorating cakes is an art form. There's no limit to what you can do with a little imagination and a lot of skill.

6: Spread frosting over entire cake

7: Add colorful candy sprinkles

8: Don't forget the candles!

Look up the hill!
It's Shelly.

She has another cake!
We're saved!

Wow. Really slowly.

Yeah, like, really...really...REALLY slowly.

She's coming
our way...slowly.

15 minutes later...

The birthday cake
has arrived!

This is a birthday cake.

2 cups of ~~flour~~ dirt

1 cup of ~~sugar~~ honeycomb

1/2 cup of ~~liquid~~ pond water

Stir ~~slowly~~ super fast for 3 minutes

~~Bake at 350 degrees for 10 minutes~~ under a duck until things get awkward...

(Continued)

Spread ~~frosting~~ mud over entire cake

Add colorful ~~candy~~ acorn sprinkles

Don't forget the ~~candles!~~ flaming twigs!

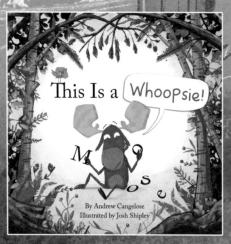

Also available in this series!